Y0-BZI-663

The Fast and Furiously Happy

Owlkids Books

Chirp, Tweet, and Squawk loved to play in their playhouse. On this particular day, they were playing...

"Race car drivers!" suggested Squawk.

"Race car drivers in their biggest race ever!" added Tweet.

"Race car drivers in their biggest, fastest race ever!" said Chirp.

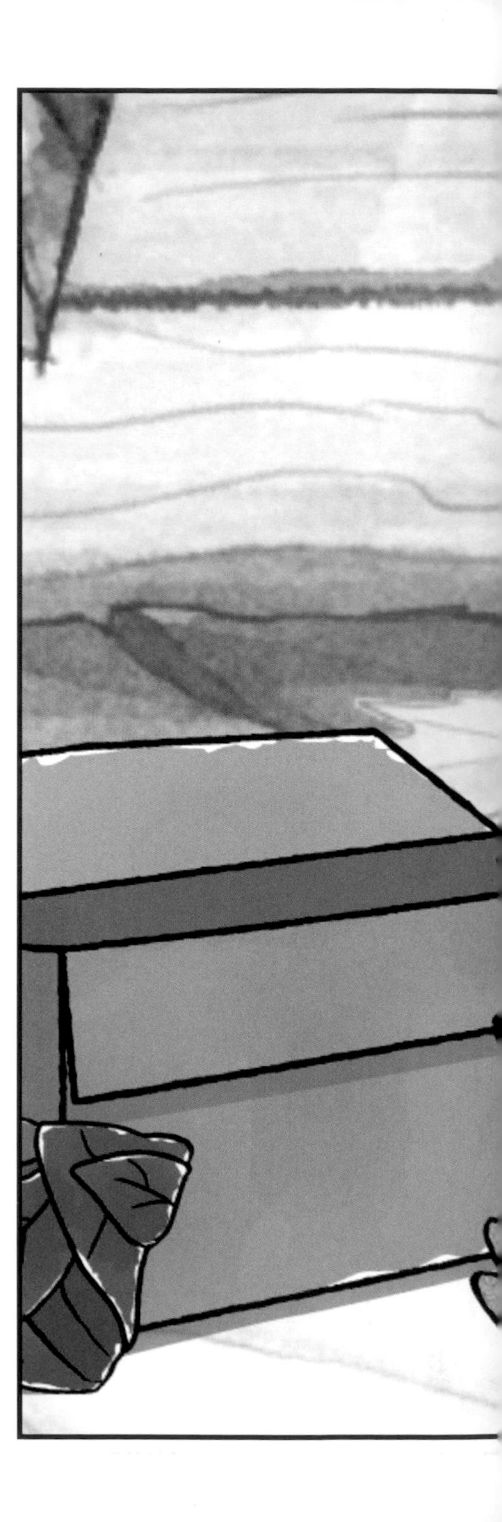

"Okay, it's my turn to drive!" said Race Car Driver Tweet.

"No! It's my turn!" said Race Car Driver Squawk.

"Stop arguing, you guys!" said Race Car Driver Chirp. "Someone is catching up to us!"

Suddenly, a red race car zoomed past Chirp, Tweet, and Squawk.

"Go, Chirp! Go!" said Tweet.

"Drive faster! Fast like the wind!" said Squawk.

"Hold on to your seats!" said Chirp.

Race Car Driver Chirp put the pedal to the metal and caught up to the red race car.

"See you later, Red Racer!" said Chirp, as he sped back into first place.

"We're winning!" cheered Tweet.

"Eat. Our. Dust," said Squawk.

ERRT!

Suddenly, they hit a giant puddle of mud and started skidding.

"Oh, no!" yelled Chirp. "We're losing control of the car!"

"Oh, no!" yelled Tweet. "We're going to crash into the side of that mountain!"

"Oh, no!" yelled Squawk. "We haven't taken turns driving yet!"

"We need something to help us stop!" said Chirp.

"Look in the glove box!" said Tweet.

"It's empty!" said Squawk.

"Not that one, Squawk!" said Tweet. "The one by the front door!"

"The box with all the helpful stuff," said Chirp.

The three friends opened the lid and looked inside.

"We've got lots of toothpicks," said Squawk.

"And a flashlight and a fan and a backpack...with a pull string?" said Tweet.

"That's no backpack," said Chirp. "That's my grandma's parachute."

"A pair of *what*?" asked Squawk.

"A parachute," said Chirp. "People use them to float high on the wind and then come down for a safe landing."

"Parachutes also help boats, planes, and even space shuttles slow down," said Tweet.

"Which is exactly what we need!" said Chirp, racing back to their car.

Race car drivers Chirp, Tweet, and Squawk were back in the race...

"Quick!" yelled Chirp. "Attach the parachute to the back of the race car!"

"Attaching!" said Squawk.

"Now pull the string!" said Tweet.

"Pulling!" said Squawk.

The parachute shot out the back of the car and brought them to a stop.

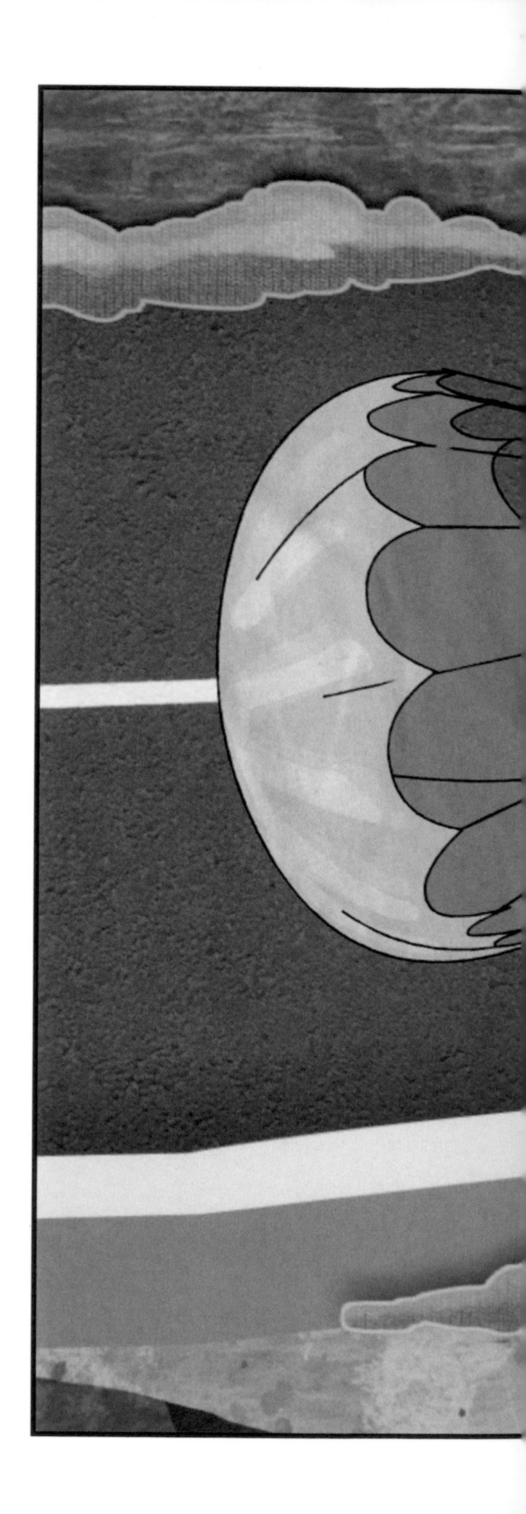

SCREECH!

"Whew!" said Chirp. "We didn't crash."

"Great," said Tweet. "But we're not going to win this race, either."

"There goes the Red Racer!" said Squawk. "She's driving fast like the wind!"

"Don't worry," said Chirp. "We can catch up! I know another route!"

But as race car drivers Chirp, Tweet, and Squawk turned a corner, they lost control of their car again!

"Ahh!" yelled Chirp. "We're going too fast!"

"Ahh!" yelled Tweet. "We're driving off the cliff!"

"Ahh!" yelled Squawk. "We're supposed to take turns driving!"

"Quick!" yelled Tweet. "Attach the parachute to the car again!"

"Attaching!" said Squawk.

"Now pull the string again!" said Chirp.

"Pulling!" said Squawk.

FWOOP!

The parachute shot up into the air and the car floated down for a safe landing. Race car drivers Chirp, Tweet, and Squawk were back in the race once again...

"Yay!" said Tweet. "There's the finish line!"

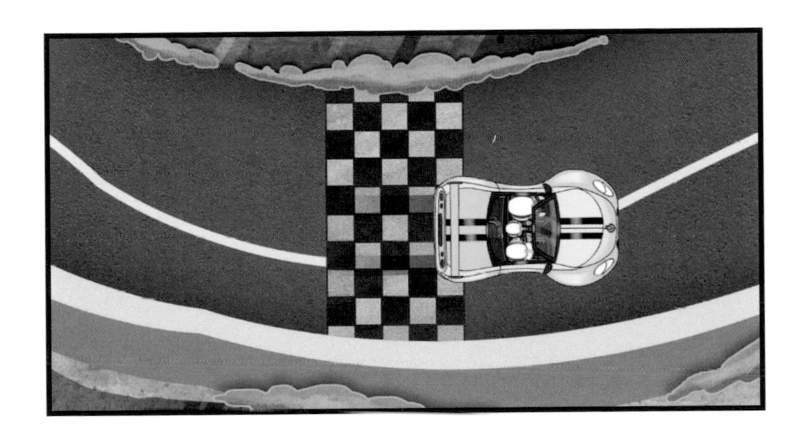

"Yay!" said Squawk. "That was close!"

"Yay!" said Chirp. "We just won the biggest, fastest race ever!"

"So, who wants to do that again?" asked Chirp.

"I do! But can it be my turn to drive?" asked Squawk.

"Sure," said Tweet. "But only if you promise to drive fast! *Fast like the wind!*"

From an episode of the animated TV series *Chirp*, produced by Sinking Ship (Chirp) Productions. Based on the Chirp character created by Bob Kain.

Based on the TV episode *The Fast and Furiously Happy* written by Nicole Demerse. Story adaptation written by J. Torres.

Owlkids Books acknowledges the financial support of the Canada Council for the Arts, the Ontario Arts Council, the Government of Canada through the Canada Book Fund (CBF) and the Government of Ontario through the Ontario Media Development Corporation's Book Initiative for our publishing activities.

Published in Canada by
Owlkids Books Inc.
10 Lower Spadina Avenue
Toronto, ON M5V 2Z2

Library and Archives Canada Cataloguing in Publication

Torres, J., 1969-, author
The fast and furiously happy / adapted by J. Torres.

(Chirp ; 6) Based on the TV program Chirp; writer of the episode Nicole Demerse.

ISBN 978-1-77147-179-4 (pbk.).--ISBN 978-1-77147-180-0 (bound)

I. Demerse, Nicole, author II. Title.

PS8589.O6755667F38 2015 jC813'.54 C2015-903658-5

Edited by: Jennifer Stokes
Designed by: Susan Sinclair

Funded by the Government of Canada
Financé par le gouvernement du Canada | Canadä

Manufactured in Altona, MB, Canada, in July 2015, by Friesens Corporation
Job #213922

A B C D E F

Publisher of Chirp, chickaDEE and OWL
www.owlkidsbooks.com

Owlkids Books is a division of